The Secret Diary of
Archie the Zuchon

by Helen Edwards

DISCLAIMER

The diary entries are fictional in that I'm imagining how my dog, Archie, views the world, though everything that happens, the various trips and so on, are true. Some names have been changed, some events have been compressed, and the order of events have been re-arranged.

To Nana Rose

xx

Contents

A note from the author

This book is all about life from a dog's perspective. How did this book come about? I was a first-time puppy parent when I got Archie. This was back in January 2016. I found the first few months stressful. Prior to getting Archie I'd done a lot of research, but nothing had prepared me for how full-on life with a young puppy would be.

I decided to write about my experience with Archie in the hope of helping other new puppy parents who were feeling overwhelmed by their pups. That became *All About Archie: Bringing Up A Puppy*. It turns out that the book helped/helps new puppy parents AND people thinking about getting a puppy.

I felt I had more to say and so I wrote a second book called *More About Archie: The Post Puppy Years*. It's about life with a young adult dog. In both books I included some comments from Archie. In *More About Archie*, Archie has a travel journal.

I love writing as Archie – it makes me smile – and the feedback I've received suggests that people want to hear more from Archie, hence this book.

If you've got a dog, I hope you can identify with some of the stories. If you're thinking about getting a dog, this book will give you some idea of what life with a dog is like. If you're a dog lover, whether you've got a dog or not, I hope this book makes you laugh, just as I have been laughing as I write it. Enjoy!

Love, Helen xx

Archie: *Mum! This is my book. I'll let you keep this section, but no more.*

A note from Archie

Hello, everyone. My name's Archie, I'm four years old, and I'm a Zuchon, which is a very friendly type of dog.

Things you should know about me. I'm really easy-going, but there are some things I hate, like wind or heavy rain, having a bath, having my beard brushed – I especially don't like that! But there are lots of things I do like, and I love, love, love sausages. Ha ha.

Licks, Archie

January

Guess what? Mum took me to the village shop today. It's a shop and a Post Office, actually. I've been in there lots of times, and the nice lady at the counter always gives me a treat.

Mum posted her parcel and I ate my treat, but on the way out I disgraced myself.

We passed a sack of potatoes, you see, and there was a lovely smell by it. I had to stop and in-ves-ti-gate. It was a message from a fellow dog (I can't tell you what it said – we dogs are allowed some secrets), and well, it would have been rude of me not to leave a reply. I cocked my leg before Mum could stop me.

She was mortified. She went up to the lady and told her what I'd done, apologising far too many times in my opinion, and offered to clean up after me.

And do you know what? The lady just laughed and told Mum another dog had done the same thing. You see? That's the only reason I did it, because you know, I'm a good boy.

She had it cleaned up in a jiffy and wouldn't hear of Mum helping. Thankfully, I hadn't wet the sack of potatoes, just the floor nearby. Phew!

Mum joked that I'd be banned from the shop, and the lady said they'd put up a "wanted" poster. Well, really!

I haven't been banned and Mum's taken me in there since then, but she held me in her arms the whole time. She's not convinced I won't do it again.

I'll try not to, Mum, but if someone leaves a message, you have to leave an RSVP, don't you? Ha ha.

Mum bought me a new coat. I refused to move until she took it off me.

Had a good day. Breakfast, a sniff round the garden, back to bed for a bit with Mum, a w.a.l.k. (I know what that means), a game of fetch, lunchtime snacks, a snooze, another sniffing session in the garden, a game of hide and seek, tea, dessert (which is some very tasty paste spread on my antler chew), a massage, another snooze, one last sniff round the garden, and biscuits at bedtime. These things happen every day, though, so every day is a good day!

Mum put me in my pjs in the middle of the day because I was still damp after my shower. I wasn't happy. To show my displeasure I jumped all over the sofa. Mum calls me buckaroo when I do that.

Today is the anniversary of the day I went to live with Mum and Dad. To celebrate we went for a new walk – round the ruins of a castle! It was cold and there was still some of the white stuff hanging round, so I wore my jumper.

There was no one else there (just how Dad likes it), and there was so much to explore. Mum and Dad seemed to spend a lot of time looking upwards at the remains of the castle walls, whilst I much preferred in-ves-ti-ga-ting at ground level.

Later, Mum made me a special tea. Yum, yum. I wish I could have chicken every day. A dog can dream, can't he?

Sorry, I can't stop. I'm going to check for post with Mum.

I saw a squirrel. She was sitting on a branch of the ha-zel-nut tree which is next to our conservatory. She looked at me through the glass. The cheek! I barked but she didn't move. It was like she had all the time in the world, sitting there, chomping on a nut; she never once took her eyes off me. When Dad came through to see what all the noise was about, the squirrel jumped onto the conservatory roof and went out of sight. Of course, it was nothing to do with Dad; it was my barking which warned her off.

I met a cat today, at the place where I go for a groom (boo!). I went up to her, all friendly like, but she didn't want to play. Instead she swiped my nose with her paw!

Mum wasn't very happy to find a little lump of poo caught in my beard. I must have picked it up on my walk. Sometimes Mum manages to stop me putting my head in long grass, but not always. I had to have my beard washed!

My favourite spot for lane-watching duty is on top of the sofa.

February

Guess what? I saw a cat on my walk. It just sat in the road looking at me. I wanted to go up to it, but Mum wouldn't let me. Boo! The only way she could get me to move past the cat was to throw some treats for me to find. I won't forget the cat, though, and I'll be keeping a lookout for it next time we go that way.

I went in a shop today. There were a lot of clothes. I'd normally be bored in a clothes shop, but there were other things in there, plus I could smell all the dogs who'd been in there, so I was kept busy.

Mum said I was a very good boy because I didn't cock my leg once. I did feel a bit silly when I jumped up at what I thought was a human, only to find it felt very different; it wasn't soft enough. Mum said it was a man-ne-quin and laughed.

She pointed out a bike she liked the look of. She told Dad she wanted a bike with a basket on it so she could take me out for rides. I closed my ears. I'm not sure I like the sound of that!

The nice lady from the supermarket came in her van. I barked until I realised it was her. She brought lots of goodies; some were even for me! And best of all, she gave me a massive fuss along with some of the treats she keeps in her van especially for all the dogs she meets. She's ace!

I like to surprise Mum by jumping on her in bed in the mornings. I get up with Dad, you see, whilst Mum has a lie-in. Sometimes she falls back to sleep, but I never let her sleep in late.

Mum went out shopping and left me behind. How dare she? But it was okay because Dad was at home and he took me out for a walk. Except … it was wet and windy, so I stopped, turned round, and led Dad home. We played fetch instead, my version of it anyway. I took Monkey in the lounge and waited for Dad to come and get him from me. Ha ha. Not long afterwards I remembered Mum was still out, so I took up my lane-watching duties.

When Mum came home I showed her just how pleased I was to see her by basically giving any part of her I could reach a good wash. And guess what? She played fetch with me, only this time Mum went to get Monkey from where I left him.

Sometimes Mum and Dad hide my kibble amongst my toys or roll it up in a blanket for me to find. They ask me to sit, shake, rollover, and wait. I'm good at waiting. Mum gets me to lie on my side and puts a piece of kibble RIGHT BY MY NOSE! I have to concentrate, but Mum never makes me wait for long, thank goodness.

Mum and Dad took me for a walk along the canal today. A woman gave me a piece of chicken. I liked her, but not her dog. He was big and in my face far too much.

We moved on and I was fas-cin-a-ted by a bridge. I stayed on it for ages, just sniffing.

I did a lot of exploring; up and down steps and slopes. I even jumped on a bench before Mum could stop me.

I had a shower when we got home because I was really dirty. I was so tired I didn't even want to play like I normally do after tea. I thought I'd give Mum and Dad some peace, for one night only. Normal service will resume tomorrow.

I could tell Dad was awake this morning, but he was just lying there, not doing anything, so I climbed on top of him. He stroked me for a bit, but then he stopped and I had to nudge him. He got up in the end, which meant I could stretch out on his side of the bed and go back to sleep. A good plan, no?

Mum says that rolling around on the bed (me, not her), at 4.30am is too early. But I felt so happy.

I saw something running across the floor. It was a lot smaller than me, yet it had more legs. How can that be? It stopped moving, so I went to take a closer look. I stared at it for what felt like ages until I heard Mum scream, 'Spider!', which made me jump. Dad had to come and catch it and take it outside.

March

Guess where Mum and Dad took me? Mum searched on the internet and found a dog café. We met Nana Val and Grandad Barry there, and it was ace. There was another dog called Archie there, so when Mum called me, she got two Archies for the price of one! Nana joked we'd gained a second dog.

Archie two (I'm number one of course), was younger than me - not quite three. He's a Cockapoo and he was full of beans. His owner said everyone thought he was still a puppy, and my mum replied that people often thought I was a puppy too because I get so excited. Except today I was nice and calm. I was kind of tired because I usually nap mid-afternoon. I couldn't nap in the café, though, there were too many things to go and in-ves-ti-gate.

I met a few dogs, some big, some small. It was lovely because I was allowed off my lead and could wander round. The café has a gate outside which has a big sign on it asking people to 'please close the gate'. I spent some time inside and outside. Mum had to come looking for me several times. Sometimes she found me with another human, having a nice stroke.

And then I got tired and spent some time on her knee, then on Dad's, then on Nana's, then on Grandad's. I like to share the love.

I ran round with Archie two for a bit. It made Mum laugh when Archie two's owner called him by his full name – Archibald. Mum and Dad call me Archibald sometimes too.

There were loads of toys to play with, and beds to sleep in.

I didn't like it when Mum went to the loo and I squeaked a bit, much to Dad's embarrassment. Some

of the other dogs barked at times, though – I didn't –
so I'm sure some squeaking's allowed.

This café definitely got the paws up from me and
the thumbs up from Mum and Dad. I think my
grandparents liked it too – Grandad got a lot of
attention from the other dogs there. Ha ha.

I was de-ligh-ted to find some bird poop on the lawn.
I tried to rub my neck in it, but Mum managed to stop
me. Boo!

Mum and Dad played a game this afternoon. Yahtzee
they said it was called. It wasn't like any of my
games. I went to in-ves-ti-gate because, you know,
I'm nosey. Mum complained I was messing the dice
up. I did it a few times (ha, ha), so in the end Dad got
my cushion and put it by the side of him. I lay on it
and had a siesta (keeping one eye on the game, of
course!)

Don't tell Mum but I don't mind having my teeth
brushed. I love the toothpaste, and if I can I lick it off
the brush before Mum's had a chance to get the brush
in my mouth.

I love, love, love crisps. I mostly get given plain ones, but sometimes Mum slips me a really tasty one, like the one she gave me today; bacon, I think she said.

I was in my nana Rose's back garden today and found some very interesting smells. They've got a squirrel who visits their garden and eats all the birdseed! He didn't visit whilst I was there, but I could smell him. I rolled on my back on one particular smelly spot. Nice! Could he be related to the squirrel I saw?

The groomer's got a dog! His name's Scamp and well, he's okay. I don't mind him. He didn't bother me too much. I was more interested in seeing the cat again, but she didn't make an appearance.

Sorry, I can't stop. I'm on duty. I've got to keep an eye on the lane. We've got a Sainsburys delivery due soon …
    …The shopping's here, but the man's been and gone. I barked at him and he left. Job done.

I love eggs, scrambled or boiled, it doesn't matter. And now I've discovered omelette. Eggs and cheese, the perfect com-bi-na-tion.

I had a long lie-in this morning. I didn't even get up to see what Mum and Dad were having for breakfast. I was lovely and comfy on the big bed and because I heard Dad say it was raining, I saw no reason to get up, not even for my own breakfast. I had what you humans call "brunch" instead.

April

Guess what? Mum and Dad took me into town today. We went to a café where they allow dogs inside. Not quite as cool as the dog café, but the nice lady at the counter gave me a biscuit, which was all right by me!

I was quite happy to lie by Dad's feet and play with the biscuit for a while. Mum and Dad seemed to take ages with their drinks, though, and I got a bit restless, so Mum put me on her lap. It meant I could see out of the window. When I saw another dog, I barked. I couldn't help it.

Mum and Dad were so embarrassed. Mum a-pol-o-gi-sed to all the other humans in the café, but they just laughed. They thought it was funny. I did too!

Mum and Dad got up to leave soon afterwards. They were stopped by a man sitting near the door. He thanked them for bringing me, saying that it was lovely to see a dog in the café. Ah!

Mum and Dad were pleased, and my heart was positively bursting.

Hopefully it won't put Mum and Dad off taking me to the café again.

Mum, Dad, I'll try to remember not to bark next time (though I can't promise I won't, it depends who I see, ha ha).

I've been sunbathing. I love, love, love lying in the grass, feeling the sun on my back. There was a slight breeze and it rustled my hair, but I didn't mind.

When Mum or Dad say 'come here' to me, and I don't want to go, I stay where I am. But when Mum adds 'I'm waiting', I know she means business. I look at her, look behind me, and because I'm a good boy, I make my way over to where she's standing, only I stop just before she can reach me. When she does reach out to me, I dart away. More often than not it turns into a game, which was my plan all along.

I saw something new today. It was small and it had spots on its back. I stared at it for ages. Then Mum came in the room and said, 'Oh, a ladybird.' She let it crawl onto her hand and then she took it outside. I was sad.

Nana Rose came to see me. I got such a surprise. I was so excited I kept jumping on and off the sofa. I barked at Nana a few times. I was just telling her how pleased I was to see her. She gives the best hugs and she always brings me sausages!

Auntie Anne came too, and Grandad Brian. I made sure to give each of them some attention. I sat on Grandad's lap and gave my paw to Auntie Anne. She takes me for walks when I go to her house.

They came with us for a walk and I showed them all my favourite sniffing spots in the lane. It was brilliant!

I played with the new toy Auntie Anne bought for me. It's a meerkat. Mum says I look like a meerkat whenever I stand on two legs.

There were some strange creatures in the field next to our house today. I've forgotten what they're called. I've seen them before but not for a long time. Mum says they've been living in a barn for the winter. Cows! That's what they're called.

One of them came up to the gate. She was too big to play with. We stared at each other for a while. I did a little dance – what Mum calls 'the moon walk'. She threw a treat for me and I ran to find it. When I looked back the cow was still looking at me.

Mum took photos of some blossom trees on our walk. I couldn't see what was so interesting about them. The poo I found was far more worthy of a pic (and a sniff).

It wasn't a good morning for me. First, Mum brushed me. Then she cleaned my teeth. Then she put drops in my ears! I know I like to be the centre of attention, but this was a bit too much. I enjoyed all the treats I was given, though, and the toothpaste's tasty, so maybe it wasn't so bad (don't tell Mum).

We went back to the castle. Mum said to Dad that she was surprised to see me jumping over walls, but they weren't very high. I wanted to in-ves-ti-gate as much as I could. Mum let me go wherever I wanted so I made the most of it. We went round the grounds twice! I had lots of messages to leave, you see.

May

Guess what? My pal from down the road, Gizmo, popped by to visit me in the garden this afternoon. He didn't wait for the gate to be opened; he pushed his way through the hedge! Crazy dog. He sniffed my bottom, I sniffed his, and then we ran round in circles for a bit.

I've got a new game: stealing Mum's slippers to get her out of bed in the morning and play with me!

I went for a groom (boo!). No sign of Scamp or the cat today. When Mum came to pick me up I was so excited. I ran to her, then I ran out of the front door and well, I just ran and ran. I could hear Mum calling me, but the freedom went to my head. I found an interesting pot to smell a few gardens down and that's when Mum caught up with me. She grabbed me and held me tight for a moment. She was out of breath!

Mum and Dad took me for a walk round the fishing pond. There was a lot of poo – geese poo, Dad said. I'm happy to report I ate a lot of it. Mum and Dad were not so happy!

We went to a new place today – something lake. Mum and Dad forgot my extendable lead, but luckily there was an old lead, a short one, in the boot of the car, so they used that. M&D really wished they'd brought the ex-ten-da-ble one because I kept them busy, pulling them here and there and everywhere! Ha ha.

I've been sick! When Dad was clearing it up he found a piece of elastic band in it. Ah, I remember when I found it outside. It was tasty. I'd eat it again.

I saw a squirrel on our walk today, except it wasn't Suzie Squirrel (that's what I've named her), it was a different one. How could I tell? Well, it had a different scent, but mostly because it was smaller than Suzie. Dad said it was a baby squirrel. Do they have names for those, I wonder? Anyway, this squirrel didn't seem at all bothered by me and Dad and stayed where it was as we approached. I made a dash for it, but it was too quick for me and disappeared into the field.

I thought Mum had forgotten about putting some tasty paste on my antler chew this evening, so I grumbled to her and she got up straightaway to get it for me. She thinks she's trained me, but I have her well trained. Ha ha.

I do love a biscuit or two before bed.

I was walking down the lane, minding my own business, when a hen ran across the road right in front of me. I couldn't believe my eyes, and of course, I had to in-ves-ti-gate. I watched the hen as it ran into someone's drive and into the back garden. I tried to follow, but Dad stopped me. He said, 'You wouldn't want to meet a hen, Archie', but I did, Dad! I still do. I waited, hoping it would come back out. I only moved away when Mum got the treats out. But I haven't forgotten, and I will be keeping a lookout.

June

Guess what? I went on an ad-ven-ture today. Mum took me to a garden centre.

Ooh – all those amazing smells. I could smell all the other dogs who'd been there, which meant I wanted to leave a few messages myself, much to Mum's embarrassment. They were only little ones.

Anyway, I loved, loved, loved the garden centre. Some people stopped to give me a fuss – they said I could probably smell their dog on them. They didn't even mind when I put my paws on their legs, though Mum tried to stop me. They said their dog's bigger than me and they're used to much worse.

Mum bought some plants and when we went to pay I met a black Labrador. We exchanged sniffs – it's the polite thing to do. I may be small, but I can hold my own with big dogs. And guess what? She rolled over and showed me her tummy. I didn't know what to make of that. Do you think that meant she liked me?

Then Mum took me home in the car. It was a hot day and she had the air-con on in the car at full blast, which I was glad of. When we arrived home and I'd cooled down a bit, Mum rubbed an ice cube all over my tummy. I love it when she does that! And then she gave me a snack, and I fell asleep on the sofa dreaming of everyone I met at the garden centre.

Sorry, I can't stop. I'm on duty. I've got to keep an eye on the lane. The postman's due soon.

Mum's set me up on Instagram and guess what? In just a couple of weeks I've got nearly the same number of followers as Mum, and she's been on the 'gram for a year. Aww!

On my walk today I made sure we passed the nice lady's house. I don't know her name, but she always makes a big fuss of me whenever she sees me. I was hoping she might be in her garden and guess what? She was! I let her know how de-light-ed I was to see her and she gave me lots of kisses and cuddles. I didn't mind how long she chatted to my mum because I was loving the attention. I didn't want to leave, but then Mum threw a treat for me to 'go find' and that was all I could think about.

Every time Mum puts her hairdryer on I run to her. I love feeling the warm air on my back, but NEVER on my face. Oh no!

Today Mum chopped some carrots. I've learnt that if I hang around the kitchen she'll eventually give me a piece of carrot or three. I love carrots! Mum says hearing me crunching them makes her smile. Win win.

Instagram update: I've now got even more followers and I've overtaken Mum. Aww!

I went out last thing with Dad. He was wearing a headtorch because it's really dark at the bottom of the garden. All of a sudden the light from the torch picked out not one, not two, but three pairs of eyes! I dashed towards them, ignoring Dad's calls, but whatever they were they disappeared into a hole underneath one of the trees. I thought about barking. I considered doing a dirt dance. I did a wee on the spot, because they were in my garden after all. Dad caught up with me, picked me up and took me back inside. Boo! I later heard him say to Mum that they were fox cubs. I hope I see them properly next time.

Success! I rolled in some bird poo. Dad wasn't happy because he had to wash me.

Downward dog? I stretch after every snooze. It's also a way we dogs show you humans affection, so give us a stroke when we stretch in front of you.

I saw the comb and knew what Mum was planning, so I hid under the purple chair (it's a great hiding place. Mum and Dad can't reach me if I stay at the back). But Mum was clever. When she left the room I thought it was safe to come out, but when I walked into the hall to see where she'd gone, she swooped down and picked me up. I'll remember that, Mum!

July

Guess where I went today? Llan, Llan, Llan something or other. What's that, Mum? Oh yes, Llangollen.

There were a lot of people around, which wasn't so great for me having to navigate all those legs, sometimes on really narrow pavements.

Plus it was warm. Mum and Dad kept stopping to give me a drink of water, and sometimes Mum poured some water on my back. I liked that.

We found a cafe down at the railway station. It looked like an old train carriage, Mum said. I was allowed inside. Neither Mum nor Dad offered me a piece of their food! Mum gave me some of my kibble and a few treats, though, so I forgave them.

Afterwards we went to walk by the canal and a boat passed us. I didn't like it and I decided to sit down in protest. Mum and Dad thought they'd have to abandon walking alongside the canal, but I changed my mind eventually. Another boat passed us. This time it was pulled by a horse! I like horses, so I forgot about the boat.

Later we had a little wander round the town centre itself. Then Mum wanted to see the steam train. I didn't know what to make of it. I know about steam, of course. Mum has this thing she uses at home to pull back and forth along the floor (why?). Sometimes I bark when a load of steam comes out.

There was a lot more steam coming from the train, though. We went down onto the platform and watched as they connected the engine to the carriages.

When the train started moving I was a bit taken aback, but I knew I was safe because Mum was holding me. I felt quite superior to the other dog on the platform, who started barking at the train and didn't stop until it was out of sight!

Dad wanted to go to some place called the Horseshoe Pass. I thought I was going to meet a load of horses, but I didn't see any, nor shoes, apart from the ones Mum and Dad were wearing. There was a lot of poo, but sheep poo doesn't interest me, much to Mum and Dad's relief. Ha ha. It was cooler there than it was in the town. I liked it. I think I'm a country dog at heart.

And then we went home and after tea I had an early night. I was ex-haus-ted. I dreamt of horses, boats, trains, and sheep poo.

Oh no! Mum's bought some of those clipper thingies. I hope they're not for me.

Mum went to do some writing in the garden. I lay on the grass beside her, listening to the birds making funny noises, feeling the sun on my back … Mum calls me her sun bunny. When she finished writing I climbed on to her lap and we had a cuddle.

I pulled out a big poo from the grass verge on my walk. Mum was NOT happy. I dropped it and she pulled me away before I could get to it again. Boo!

Mum used the clipper thingies on me. She said she's trying to keep me tidy between grooms. She gave me loads of treats, so I didn't mind standing still for a while, but then I got bored and she stopped.

I saw Suzie Squirrel again. She was sitting eating what Mum said was a ha-zel-nut in my back garden. I ran as fast as I could, but I was too late. Suzie went up a tree. I wish I could do that. I did find the shell she left behind, and very tasty it was indeed. Mum wasn't happy about me eating it, but what's a dog to do? It was nice and crunchy.

My pal, Gizmo joined, us at one point on our walk today. Mum gave him one of my treats! But then she gave me one. In fact, she asked us both to sit and wait. I watched whilst Gizmo ate his treat, and he watched whilst I ate mine. Mum said we were good boys.

Dad decided to take me through some fields on our walk. There were cows, and one came over to us. I wasn't keen. Dad picked me up.

A parcel came for me today. It had my name on it (and Mum's). I sniffed the box then let Mum open it. Inside there were some lovely treats – all for me! Of course I had to have one there and then. Duck flavoured – my favourite. I'm licking my lips just thinking about them.

I saw the hen again. It popped out onto the road, then turned and ran back down the drive. Once again, I was too late. Pesky lead. I wish Mum and Dad would let me loose, but they don't trust me to stay close to them (they're right not to trust me by the way, but don't tell them that).

August

Guess what? I went to Ellen and Ned's house today. It's the new doggy daycare place my mum found. Ellen gave me lots of cuddles. Any time she sat down I was straight in there. Ha ha. And Ned's cool – my sort of dog. He's not in your face like some dogs are.

I had a good old sniff round the house and the garden, and I even ran round with Ned at one point. Then I met Lily. She's a youngster and she's tiny! I helped her as much as I could.

When Lily went home Ellen took me and Ned for a lovely walk across the fields in the sunshine. When we got back, I had a snack and then I did some sunbathing in the garden until it was time for Mum and Dad to pick me up. I had a great time, but I always love to go home. I was so tired I slept most of the evening. Mum and Dad were de-ligh-ted!

The clipper thingies are coming out far too often for my liking. Mum says she has to do it in stages, because I get bored and start moving around.

A bee stung me. I held up my paw and Mum carried me back inside (we'd just started our walk).

Mum checked my paw but the sting must have fallen out. She bathed my paw anyway and put an ice cube on it. I felt tired so I had a bit of a snooze and when I woke up I ate a bit of plain omelette. Not long afterwards I was rolling around on the sofa and Mum said I must be all right.

I didn't miss out on my walk. We went in the evening for a change.

I don't like bees.

For the record, Mum, I prefer it when Dad showers me. It doesn't take so long, and he doesn't clean under my eyes afterwards.

Nana Val and Grandad Barry visited me today. I was so excited to see them. Nana brought me treats (she can come again). I don't know what they were, only that they didn't smell very interesting. Mum said they were pieces of dried sweet potato. I wasn't impressed. Bring better treats next time, Nana!

Once I'd calmed down I was tired, so I had a nap on Mum's chest. She smelt nice. Ap-pa-rent-ly I used to do that a lot when I was a pup, and I still do it every now and then, but only with Mum.

Mum and Dad had scrambled egg on toast for tea. For one horrible moment I thought they'd forgotten to leave me some egg. I paced and I paced, but I needn't have worried. They wanted the egg to cool before they gave it to me. Hurray!

I saw a frog. It was when I went out for one last sniff and a wee before bedtime. I thought it was a leaf at first, only it didn't smell like one. I sniffed the grass round it for a bit and then I put my nose right by it, close but not touching. It moved! But I wasn't deterred. Oh no! I followed it, and I would have kept on following it had Dad not called me in. But then again, a biscuit was waiting for me.

We went to a garden centre today, but it didn't just sell plants. There were lots of other things in the shop that Mum wanted to look at. I could have gone in, but I'm not keen on shopping, so Dad and me went for a walk outside.

Then we went to the café. Mum and Dad had some cake. I would have liked some of that, but Mum gave me a few of my treats instead. I had to sit quiet and wait before she gave me one, though.

She wanted me to calm down, you see. Both Mum and Dad got really embarrassed for some reason because I was making squeaky noises. I can't help it when I'm excited. There were new sounds and scents and people! I wanted to go and say hello to everyone.

The other humans didn't seem to mind. They smiled and came up to me and stroked me. They told Mum and Dad how gorgeous I am and that my hair's so soft. Mum and Dad liked that. I did too!

I went for a groom (boo!). I saw the cat again, but only briefly. She was just on her way out. Cats seem to be able to go where they like. Why can't dogs do that? Mind you, I wouldn't want to leave Mum and Dad for too long.

Dad had tuna today but he didn't share any with me. Maybe next time.

I saw a butterfly. It was lying in the road. It wasn't moving and I think Mum thought it was dead, only when I nudged it with my nose (I was only in-ves-ti-gat-ing) it moved and made me jump. I could only watch as it flew away. It must have just been having a rest, like I do when I'm tired.

September

Guess where I've been? A cool restaurant called Hickory's, where they have a special dog-friendly section inside.

I've been there a few times now because Mum and Dad meet Nana Rose and Grandad Brian and Auntie Anne there sometimes for a meal. They all love the waffles. I don't know what the waffles are like because I've never been offered any (how rude), but Nana makes up for it by feeding me bits of sausage from her handbag. I love my nana.

And I love Hickory's. The staff always make a fuss of me. Today the nice lady brought me a biscuit, which Mum didn't think I'd eat because I'm fussy where dog biscuits are concerned, but after a thorough investigation I decided to eat it, and then another one!

The humans' talk went over my head. I was more interested in a puppy who came in not long after us. I pulled on my lead a bit to let Mum know I wanted to go and say hello, so she took me over. I had a good sniff and the puppy – a girl – sniffed my bum.

Then I went back to Nana and she gave me some more sausage. Mum always tells her to only give me a couple of pieces (I get a lot more than that – more like two whole sausages – but sshh! It's a secret).

I snoozed on the blanket Mum brought for me, but I soon jumped to attention when they got up to leave. Time for a w.a.l.k.!

Grandad walked me for a bit. That's never happened before. I made the most of it and led him to places he hadn't been planning on going. Ha ha.

When we passed the restaurant on our way back to the car I turned to go back inside. Everyone laughed!

I was tired when it was time to go home, so I lay down in my box on the back seat of the car. I can't wait for my next ad-ven-ture.

I went for my first sleepover at Ellen and Ned's. Ellen's cool because she lets me sleep on her bed. I jumped on her in the morning and licked her face to show my appreciation.

I kept a close eye on Mum when she put some sunflower seeds out for the birds this morning. A few dropped on the grass and I was quick to snaffle them. Tasty! Mum used to scatter them all on the ground, but when she realised I was eating them she put them somewhere higher up. She says they affect my number twos. I don't know what she means.

I heard Dad say that a cat had done a massive poo in our back garden, only I didn't get to in-ves-ti-gate because Dad scooped it up and put it in the bin before I could get to it. Boo!

I do love a bit of scrambled egg, as you know, and I get some every time Mum and Dad have it, but one night I thought they'd forgotten. I usually get mine after they've eaten, only this time Mum gave me mine to have whilst they were eating theirs. I forgot!

Hurray! Dad put a bit of tuna in my bowl. Yum yum. I love my dad.

I found Suzie Squirrel eating the sunflower seeds Mum put out for the birds. I tried to tell her the seeds weren't for her. She looked down at me from the birdseed table for one long moment, then jumped into the tree. I'm getting a bit fed up of her doing that.

Mum clipped my nails. Dad was there too, trying his best to keep me still. I didn't like it. It was made slightly better by all the treats I was given.

When Mum or Dad put on a certain pair of trousers I know we're going for a walk. I can tell from the scent of the trousers. Except Mum dis-con-cer-ted me today by taking the trousers off and putting on a different pair. But even though she was wearing a different pair of trousers, we still went on a walk. Hurray.

Frog was out again this evening. He was so still, I thought he was dead, but then he hopped and Mum screamed. Aww! Poor Mum.

I got really close to the hen today. It had to run past me in order to get home. It was taller than me. I just stood there, staring. Afterwards I had a good sniff along the grass verge where the hen had been. Hens are strange!

October

Guess what? Mum took me for a walk in the village today. The pavements were covered in yellow leaves. There were – I can't count – a lot of leaves. Mum said how pretty they looked. As for me, I did a poo right by the bin, which Mum was pleased about. I'm a good boy, you know.

I liked the sound the leaves made as I walked over them. It was like a rustling sound. And I enjoyed sticking my nose in amongst them to see what they were hiding, but I was disappointed not to find anything. Whenever I do that in the lanes near where I live, I nearly always find something another dog has left behind, and if I like the smell, I have a nibble.

Mum and Dad grumble that they can't see other dogs' poo because of the leaves. They don't like me eating poo and pull me away from it whenever they can, but I've got a big ad-van-tage. I smell poo before they spot it, so if I'm quick I can grab a bite.

Mum was trying to clip the hair on my chest. She put me on my back and I just felt so happy that I started rolling around. It made Mum laugh. Oh no! I've just realised. Now she must think I like the clipper thingies.

I went paddling today in a lake with a funny name. Mum couldn't believe it when I went in the water volun-tar-i-ly. I only did it because it was hot – it felt like summer. I was glad of the chance to cool down. I didn't go in that far. Just up to my ankles. The water was so still, and we were surrounded by mountains. Mum came in the water too.

I've been on my holidays. Mum and Dad went to Scotland without me (boo!) and I went to stay at Ellen's. Actually, I wasn't too fussed about Mum and Dad leaving me because I love going to Ellen's, plus I don't like long car journeys.

I had a brilliant week. I met lots of different dogs. They were all friendly but knew when I wanted some quiet time. I explored new places on our walks. I especially loved the evening times when I cuddled up with Ellen on the sofa. I didn't even mind the bath she gave me at the end of my holiday because she said I was a lot dirtier than when I arrived. I fell asleep on her when she was brushing me. It was very relaxing. Ooh, I almost forgot. A tractor passed the house and just as I was telling it to go away, Ned took Monkey!

I was glad to see Mum and Dad, though. I fell asleep in Mum's arms. And they brought me a cool new toy – a koala.

Dad made Mum laugh when he said my nose was on turbo. We were playing 'go find'. I do love to sniff!

Mum's bought me this thing. It's like a cushion, and it's got a bee sticking out of each of the three holes. Not real bees, thankfully. I have to remove the bees from the holes to get to the treats, only it's easier just to move the cushion. Ha ha.

Mum's just put some smelly stuff on my paws. I suppose it does make my pads feel soft, but I don't think much of the taste.

When I jumped on Mum in bed this morning I gave her a big lick on her chin. I'd just had my breakfast. She groaned and said I smelt of beef. There are worse things to smell of!

It was raining this evening when I was due to go out for one last wee. I stopped at the door, sniffed, and turned right back round. Only Mum and Dad had other ideas. They didn't want me waking them in the middle of the night, wanting a wee, so Dad came out too, and held an umbrella over me. I love my dad.

Sorry, I can't stop. I'm on duty. I've got to keep an eye on the lane because I can hear the clip-clop of horses' hooves. I like horses, but I don't like their poo.

November

Guess what? It's my birthday today so Mum and Dad took me to a stately home, although we didn't go inside. We explored the grounds instead. It was ace!

I made Mum and Dad laugh by scampering up some steps. They wanted to take my photo when I was at the top, but they had to be quick – I had some exploring to do.

We walked along paths, through fields and woods, and even in a special type of garden; a walled garden, Mum said.

We played 'go find' along the paths, and I saw loads of other dogs; some were more friendly than others.

I didn't see any deer in the Deer Park, although I heard Mum and Dad say they could see some in the distance.

When I saw a squirrel (it wasn't Suzie), I forgot I was tired and I tried to run after it, pulling Dad along with me. I couldn't catch the squirrel, though – it went up a tree!

On the way back to the car Mum and Dad stopped for a drink and some cake. I had a drink of water and the rest of my treats. I tried to get on Mum's lap, but she wouldn't let me because she said I was filthy. What's a bit of mud between friends?

I had to have a shower when I got home. And then it was time for a nice long snooze. In the evening Mum gave me some shepherd's pie. A birthday treat, she said. I love my mum.

Mum bought me something, a bow tie, she said. She wanted to take a photo of me wearing it, but I don't like my photo being taken because of that black thing Mum holds up in front of me. Today she tried something different and held a treat in one hand and the black thing in the other. I stared at the treat whilst she took some photos. She was pleased with them because I didn't turn my head. And I was pleased because I got treats (more than one actually). Clever Mum!

I took Mum round a fishing lake. I saw some funny birds on the lake and I didn't know what to make of them. Mum bent down beside me and told me they were geese. So that's where the poo came from. They didn't get out of the water, though, and I decided not to bark at them.

On the way home we met a few people who gave me a fuss. I met some dogs too. I would have played with them if I hadn't been on my lead, but Mum doesn't trust me to come back when she calls. She's right; sometimes there are things I need to in-ves-ti-gate. My fellow dogs will understand.

Suzie Squirrel was in the lane today. I wondered if she was playing 'go find' because she was searching for something in the grass. I pulled Mum along (she had the lead quite short because she was trying to stop me from getting to all the poo in the grass verges), and we got very close before Suzie scam-per-ed off. All I could do was watch as her bushy tail went further and further up the tree.

The wind made my hair stand up on end. I didn't like it so I took Dad home. I've never liked the wind, not since I was a young pup. I'd sit down on the pavement and Mum had to carry me home. I may be small (and I was even smaller then), but I'm difficult to move when I decide I don't want to.

Windy again! This storm is getting boring.

The wind's gone. Hurray! We went on a long walk to make up for the past few days. The ground was still wet, so I got really dirty, not that I care about that. I saw the nice lady again and she gave me a massive fuss.

The wind's back. I didn't even leave the garden. I went to the back door to let Dad know there wasn't going to be a walk today. We played hide and seek inside. We also did some training, in that I trained

Mum and Dad to give me treats. See? I'm a clever dog.

The wind's gone. I'll take Dad for a walk then.

I went for a groom. Boo! But. The groomer gave Mum a bag of biscuits. They're for me for Christmas ap-pa-rent-ly.

I met Dolly. She's nine months old – just a pup. She was a bit too lively for my liking. I let her sniff me but then I stood back. Mum gave her one of my treats!

December

Guess who I met today? Santa Paws! He was ace. He was sitting on a large chair and I didn't wait to be asked – I just jumped on his lap. He gave me a cuddle and asked me what I wanted for Christmas. I didn't have to think. I told him I wanted a new antler chew. He said that could easily be arranged and that I might even get one from one of his reindeers because they shed their antlers every year. And do you know what else he told me? That they grow new antlers. Amazing! He gave me another cuddle and told me I was a good boy. We had our photo taken together and then Mum came to get me, but before she took me away, Santa Paws gave me a squeaky ball. I was de-ligh-ted with it. Mum and Dad not so much.

I hope Santa's right, that I'll get a new antler chew for Christmas. He must be – he's Santa Paws!

The Christmas tree is up. I heard Dad grumbling when he was getting it from the loft. Mum spent ages decorating it. She seemed to get stressed putting the lights on it.

When I was a pup I was curious about all the things hanging from the branches. I'm a grown-up now though, so I sniffed a few things and then went back to my basket.

I've got a new bed! It was supposed to be a Christmas present, but when Mum pulled it out of the bag to check it, I couldn't resist having a nose. And I had to climb in to test it out. It was so comfy I stayed in it for the rest of the afternoon. Mum said I might as well keep it now.

I think Mum was hoping I'd love this basket so much that I'd sleep in it at night and not jump on her bed. I do love my new basket, but I love sleeping with my mum and dad even more. Sorry, not sorry, Mum.

I went to play with Ellen and Ned. Ellen thought she'd take us on a walk, but it was windy. And you know what I think about wind. We turned back and Ellen gave me my carrot toy with treats inside it to find. A much better idea!

When Mum and Dad came to pick me up, I ran straight through Mum's legs to get to Dad. I think she was a bit sad about that so I ran back to her and gave her extra licks.

I don't like bananas. Mum tries me with a piece every so often and I'll have a sniff, but nah, they're not for me. But. I do like banana cake. Mum will only give me a small piece. Boo!

Me and Dad went into town. He took me for a walk round before we went to the florists, where he bought a funny looking plant – an Or-chid, he said. It's a Christmas present for Mum. I don't understand Christmas. All I know is that there'll be lots of presents and that I'll get a special dinner, which is all right by me. Soon we were on our way back to the car. I was glad it was just the one shop. There were a lot of people around, and I don't like shopping. Like Dad, like dog!

Sorry, I can't stop. I'm on duty. I've got to keep an eye on the lane. Santa Paws is on his way!
Mum put out some carrots. They're not for the reindeers – they're for me!

Santa Paws was right. I got a new antler for Christmas. Mum wrapped it in a blanket for me to find. It didn't take me long – Dad helped me out a bit – and as soon as I could I grabbed it and lay down to have a good old chew. Yum yum.

What a day. Dad took me for a walk, and when we got back there were some lovely smells coming from the kitchen. Mum put together a little dinner especially for me! I love my mum. It was so tasty, I even ate the piece of broccoli she put in there. Don't try that too often, Mum.

I must have been a good boy because there were lots of presents with my name on them – a whole bag full. I tested out all the toys and sampled the treats. There were some very tasty biscuits. Dad said they stank of fish. I don't know about that, only that they were so tasty I had to have two.

I helped Mum and Dad with their presents too, but they weren't as interesting as mine. I know I'm lucky, and that not every dog has as many toys as me, which is why Mum will be taking some of the toys I don't play with to our local dog rescue centre in the New Year. As long as she doesn't take Monkey!

We had some visitors. Auntie Kath, Uncle Steve, and my cousins, Alys and Nia. I don't see them very often, so it was ace to get some cuddles from them. In fact, this was the first time I'd met Uncle Steve, so I made sure to give him plenty of attention and to test out whether he's allergic to me. He can't be because I'm a hyper, hypo – Mum, can you help? Hypoallergenic, that's it. I'm a hypoallergenic dog.

Do you know? Nia used to be scared of me. Yes, little old me, when all I ever try to do is lick her. Well, she's not scared anymore because you'll never guess what? Today she let me sit on her knee!

Alys gave me lots of cuddles, whilst Auntie Kath kept on stroking me and saying how soft and fluffy I am. They can come again.

Mum wanted to go on a new walk today. She said it was the last day of the year, but what that had to do with our walk, I don't know. We went to a big park. I loved it. Mum couldn't believe how fast I was on the steps, going up AND down. She was glad Dad was holding my lead. We seemed to go round in a circle, a path round a field. There were lots of places to explore – too many for one visit, so I hope we go back there soon.

I met some other dogs and their humans. Then we came to a big muddy puddle. Well, it was a puddle to Mum and Dad, but it was like a river to me. I think I would have been sucked in if I'd tried to walk in it, but Mum carried me. Hers and Dad's boots were covered in mud afterwards, whereas I remained as white as that white stuff which comes down every now and then. Ha ha. Happy New Year!

Another note from Archie

I hope you've enjoyed reading my diary. Guess what? If you go to the gall-er-y you'll see some photographs of me. Mum said you'd probably like to see what I look like. Do you? Yeah, you probably do.

I can smell something. It's coming from the kitchen. I must go and in-ves-ti-gate.

See ya,

Archie

Aka Prince Archie
Archibald
Little Man
Short Stuff
The Furry One
Babba
The Guvnor

Gall-er-y

I LOVE, LOVE, LOVE THIS
CAFE. THE NICE LADY
GIVES ME BISCUITS.

THE SOFA IS MINE!

I LOVE, LOVE, LOVE
TO SUNBATHE.

JUST BACK FROM MY GROOM.

SOMEWHERE IN LLANGOLLEN.

DO YOU LIKE MY BOW TIE?

HAS SANTA PAWS BEEN YET?

Acknowledgements

I would like to take this opportunity to thank my beta readers, Anne Hamilton, Renee McCormick, and Karen Loughran. Your input has been the icing on the cake. Thank you.

Thank you to Helen Pryke for proofreading this book. Your attention to detail never ceases to amaze me.

A big thank you to all the supporters of the Archie books. I'm still receiving messages from new puppy parents who have been helped by reading my story, which is amazing. I like to think Archie is leaving a wonderful legacy.

Thanks to my husband, Simon, for just being you, and for sorting out the last minute issues with the cover.

Archie, thank you for choosing me and Simon. Love you!

xx

About the author

Originally from North Wales, Helen currently lives in Shropshire with her husband and their Zuchon, Archie. Helen worked for many years in the public sector and has an administrative background. She writes both fiction and non-fiction. As well as being an indie author, Helen is a self-publishing assistant, offering editorial, self-publishing, and writing services.

Helen can more often than not be found daydreaming, or with her head stuck in a book. She loves the Scottish Highlands, crisps, pizza, taking photographs, and anything sparkly.

To find out more about both Helen and Archie please go to:

Website: www.helen-edwards.co.uk
Facebook www.facebook.com/ArchietheZuchon/
Instagram @archiethezuchon
Twitter @helibedw

If you enjoyed this book, and have a minute to spare, your help in spreading the word by way of a short review on Amazon would be greatly appreciated.

Also by Helen Edwards

All About Archie: Bringing Up A Puppy

Are you thinking about getting a puppy? Have you just brought home your furry friend and are feeling overwhelmed, anxious, or just plain exhausted? You're not alone.

There's no doubt your new best friend is going to be cute, funny, loveable, and hard work!

In this book Helen shares her experience of bringing up her puppy, Archie, because knowing what to expect is half the battle.

Available in e-book, paperback and audiobook format from Amazon.

E-book also available from Apple Books, Barnes & Noble, Kobo, Tolino, & Vivlio.

Audiobook also available via audible and iTunes.

More About Archie: The Post Puppy Years

It's a dog (owner's) life – isn't it? Are you a new puppy or dog parent? Is your furry friend challenging at times? Dogs bring with them a lot of fun and love, but they certainly need a lot of attention.

In this follow-up to *All About Archie: Bringing Up A Puppy*, Helen shares her experiences of living with her young dog, Archie. You'll also hear from other puppy and dog parents about the reality of life with their new best friend. And not forgetting Archie himself, who wants to add a little doggy perspective.

Available in e-book, paperback and audiobook format from Amazon.

Audiobook also available via audible and iTunes.

The Archie Collection:
Bringing Up A Puppy &
The Post Puppy Years

Helen Edwards

The Archie Collection: Bringing Up A Puppy & The Post Puppy Years

Are you thinking about getting a puppy? Have you just brought home your furry friend and are feeling overwhelmed, anxious, or just plain exhausted? You're not alone. There's no doubt your new best friend is going to be cute, funny, loveable, and hard work!

Knowing what to expect is half the battle. In this collection, Helen shares her experience of bringing up her Zuchon puppy, Archie, as well as revealing what life is like with a young adult dog as Archie grows. You'll also hear from other puppy and dog parents, and not forgetting Archie himself, who wants to add a little doggy perspective.

The Archie Collection combines the previously published All About Archie: Bringing Up A Puppy, and More About Archie: The Post Puppy Years, and includes new interviews, new stories from Archie, plus new photographs!

**Available in e-book and paperback format
from Amazon.**

Printed in Great Britain
by Amazon

17801000R00041

God's Amazing Machine

God's Amazing Machine

How Your Body Works and
Why God Designed it That Way

By Dr. Chris Cormier, D.C.

First Edition
10 9 8 7 6 5 4 3 2

Book Cover design by Cathi Stevenson
www.bookcoverexpress.com

Book Edited by Maura Leon

Interior Design by Rudy Milanovich

God's Amazing Machine (soft cover)
978-0-9851333-3-7

Dr. Chris Cormier
Lafayette, Louisiana
www.NerveHealth.com

What people are saying about *God's Amazing Machine*:

"*God's Amazing Machine* delivers a much-needed message about the relationship between God, ourselves, and health. I look forward to sharing this book with my children and participating in the well-thought-out exercises and discussions in the book. Every spiritual youth program should have this book!"

— Dr. Elizabeth Hesse Sheehan, DC, CCN, QN

"Using scripture, scientific knowledge, and personal life experiences, Dr. Chris and *God's Amazing Machine* will teach you how to have a healthy and happy life."

— Rev. Les DeMarco, Minister,
Spiritual Workshop Leader,
and Life Coach at RevLesDemarco.com

"*God's Amazing Machine* is a powerful guide to reprogram your mind and body. It offers a program that is both easy to understand and easy to implement."

— Marci Shimoff, N.Y. Times Bestselling Author
of *Happy for No Reason, Love For No Reason,*
and *Chicken Soup for the Woman's Soul*

"Put *God's Amazing Machine* to work for you! Dr. Chris Cormier teaches and reminds us of the Universal Principles of Love and Healing that can be shared with family and friends of all ages. The discussion and workbook sections allow for discovery beyond one's own experience. It is a great opportunity to share and explore your Nervous System from a new perspective in *God's Amazing Machine*."

— Dr. George Gonzalez, DC, QN,
Founder of Quantum Neurology®
Nervous System Rehabilitationand
Author of the *Holographic Healing*® Series

"Dr. Chris has done a great job with this book. The Introduction alone will teach you one of life's most important lessons. Buy two books, and give one to your best friend. They will thank you many times."

— Bob Proctor, Author and
Teacher in the movie, *The Secret*

"Get inspired to make good choices and live more healthfully, vibrantly, and youthfully with the tips and advice that Dr. Chris Cormier shares in his new book, *God's Amazing Machine*."

— Dr. Joe Vitale, Multiple Bestselling Author and
Featured Teacher in the movie, *The Secret*

"God's Amazing Machine is a practical guide that will get you in touch with how to care for the magnificent body that God has given to you."

— Rev. Emile Gauvreau, Spiritual Leader
and Bestselling Contributing Author in the book,
YOU Make a Difference

"This is a quick, easy, faith-centered and fact-centered read that cannothelp but contribute to people having a greater understandingand appreciation of their own greatest healing potential."

— Dr. Steve Hoffman, Expert in health development,
Bestselling Author and President of
Discover Wellness, Inc.

"God's Amazing Machine is filled with valuable tips and strategies to get your body back to its original, naturally-healthy state."

— Lissa Coffey, Author,
What's Your Dharma?
Discover the Vedic Way to Your Life's Purpose

"*God's Amazing Machine* is a great piece of writing. The bottom line in life is that our health is our responsibility, not something we can delegate to others."

— Rev. Dee L. Workman, USDA Inspector and Author of the books, *Daily Meds: Enriching Yourself Through Daily Devotion, The Book of Poetic Prayers: Transcending the Ordinary, and Meditation: Follow Your Bliss*

"*God's Amazing Machine* takes complex concepts of quantum physics and healing and presents them in a way that everyone can understand and use."

— Dr. Joe Rubino, Creator, HighSelfEsteemKids.com, LifeOptimizationCoaching.com and TheSelfEsteemBook.com

"Your future and purest connection to Spirit is contained within these pages. Dr. Chris has laid out a clear and easy roadmap of the nervous system, and now it's up to you to use it."

— Warren Henningsen, International Bestselling Author of the book, *If I Can You Can: Insights of an Average Man*

"Through the application of quantum physics principles, Dr. Chris is demonstrating a command of the nervous system never seen before. You have never read a book like this one!"

— Eva Gregory, America's Divine Guidance Coach and co-author of *Life Lessons for Mastering The Law of Attraction* with Jack Canfield

"An empowering blend of spirituality and gratitude, this book clearly shows how we can nurture and nourish our physical, emotional, and mental states."

— Ronny Prasad, Author of the International Bestseller, *Welcome to Your Life: Simple Insights for Your Inspiration and Empowerment*

"Dr. Chris defines our existence and reality in a way that makes sense, and gives us real tools that will empower us for the rest of our lives."

— Keith Leon, Multiple Bestselling Author, Publisher, and Book Mentor

"A must read for anyone who is serious about embracing a natural approach to an improved life — at any age."

— Ester Nicholson, Teacher, Speaker, and Author of *Soul Recovery: 12 Keys to Healing Addiction*

"Dr. Cormier's book gets to the heart of the matter of what it takes to live a happy, healthy life...a life you love because it is filled with love. His insights, tips, and exercises can transform your life starting the moment you read it!"

— Pat Finn, TV Producer and Game Show Host
of *The Joker's Wild* and *Shop 'til You Drop*

"Dr. Chris brings information together in a holistic manner, feeding our body, mind, and spirit."

— Dr. Chase Hayden, Chiropractor,
Quantum Neurologist™,
and Applied Clinical Nutritionist

"*God's Amazing Machine* will blow your mind! Finally, a clear explanation of the connection between our physical bodies and energetic bodies!"

— Dr. Adam Arnold, Chiropractor, Quantum
Neurologist™, and Quit Smoking in 60 Minutes
Specialist

"Dr. Cormier gives you information in a concise and easy-to-read format. His book will help you to create the health and life you have been searching for."

—Dr. Maureen M. Sullivan, Q.N., PhD Holistic Nutrition

"*God's Amazing Machine* provides a seven-week curriculum that emphasizes the importance of nourishing, supporting, and stimulating our brains, eating real food, and setting and achieving goals. Dr. Chris is an inspiration!"

— Dr. Edward R. Chauvin, Chiropractor, Quantum Neurology® Practioner and Author of the book, *I'm Worried Sick About My Health: How to Get and Stay Healthy Without Spending a Fortune*

"This book will assist you in re-connecting to the threefold nature of God: Body, Mind, and Spirit!"

— Dr. W.W. Beck, DC, QN, Seminar Leader and Author of the book, *21ˢᵗ Century Chiropractic*

Contents

Preface

A Message to Teachers

I want to express my sincere appreciation to every teacher and educator in the world. My wife is a teacher by profession, and I witnessed, firsthand, her arduous hours of school and student teaching prior to beginning her teaching career. Once she started teaching, I saw how hard she worked to change, for the better, the lives of all her students. I know what a daunting task this is for teachers because in order to be effective, you must adapt your teaching techniques to accommodate the many differences that exist among your students.

Many children and adults have lost appreciation for God's gift of their human bodies. Many have lost faith in their bodies' healing capacity.

Perhaps they haven't been taught properly how to take care of their bodies. This is where I come in. I want to teach every one of you the proper way to appreciate and take care of the magnificent body that God has given to you.

At the end of each chapter, you'll find a series of questions followed by a couple of exercises related to the material in the chapter. The questions are provided to stimulate oral discussion, but could also be assigned as written exercises. Please feel free to utilize or change any number of the discussion questions to fit your teaching style. The exercises below the questions are intended for students to do on their own and then share with the group, if desired. You may choose to create different presentations of the exercises with your class, whereby your students might draw a picture, compose a Tweet or musical jingle, or make up a public service announcement.

As a teacher, you are one of the blessed people offering time, passion, money, and effort in molding children to become well-adjusted adults. If you have suggestions on how to enhance the exercises and questions I have written in this book, I invite and encourage your input through the contact information on my website, www. NerveHealth.com.

Acknowledgments

First and foremost, I would like to thank God for placing me on Earth and giving me the extraordinary gift of helping people to heal themselves through the power of their nerves. The most fascinating thing about working on the human body each day is realizing that it is, truly, the most remarkable invention ever created. Thank You, God, for giving me my amazing machine and for allowing me to thrive off of the talents and abilities and resources that You gave to me. Thank You for also giving me a profession that really isn't work; it is sincere fun every day. Finally, thanks for the greatest gift of all: giving me the knowledge and resources to keep my family and myself healthy.

Words cannot express my sincere gratitude to my amazing wife, Missy, and our children, Hayden, Molly, and Lucas, for always being there for me throughout this incredible journey. Without their intuition, support, and constructive criticism, the concepts presented in this book may never have come to fruition.

I also would like to thank my thousands of patients for their unwavering support and for trusting in me to give them the highest level of care possible.

Additionally, I would like to thank my amazing office staff for their support and tireless efforts to help our patients enjoy a higher quality of life.

I also want to thank my parents for bringing me into this world and for raising me in an environment that allowed me to form an incredible relationship with God.

I would also like to thank Dr. George Gonzalez, the founder of Quantum Neurology®, for opening my eyes to a new way of taking care of the body through empowering the nervous system.

My sincere gratitude also goes to Dr. Edward Chauvin, my good friend and fellow Quantum

Neurologist™ in Abbeville, Louisiana, for choosing which Scriptures to include in the book and for introducing me to Quantum Neurology® as well.

Thanks to Dr. James Sheen, my good friend and fellow Quantum Neurologist™ in Kearney, Nebraska, for profoundly expanding my knowledge in too many areas to mention.

Thank you to all the leaders and staff at Nature's Liquids for your unwavering support and for allowing me to invent products that people need so desperately.

Thanks to Pastor Joel Osteen for being my inspiration to write about the importance of being thankful for what you have. His teaching about this was tremendously eye opening for me, and it literally changed my life.

Words cannot express my sincere gratitude to Mary Demarest, my mother-in-law, who has graciously offered her writing expertise and help with this book and my other book, The Hidden Diagnosis.

Finally, I would like to thank Keith and Maura Leon for providing their incredible writing talents in helping to get everything out of my brain and into this book in a fashion that allows people everywhere to understand the power of God's Amazing Machine through the lens of the nervous system.

Introduction

When you wake up each morning, what is the first thing you think about? Is it different every day, or is it pretty much the same? Is it a positive thought or a negative thought?

My name is Dr. Chris Cormier, and I can honestly tell you that I wake up thankful every day. I'm thankful for my family and friends, thankful for my health and well-being, and thankful that I'm able to keep helping people through the work that I do as a chiropractic physician, Quantum Neurology® practitioner, health product formulator, and published author.

But it wasn't always easy for me. I've had challenges that made me question whether I should even try.

When I was nine years old, I was fortunate enough to be one of the better baseball players in my league, and after a really good season, I got selected for the all-star team. It seemed like such a great opportunity, but for some reason, the coach decided that he didn't want to play me.

He never even gave me a chance. Throughout almost the entire all-star season—even during practice—he would, literally, sit me on the bench and not even practice me.

I had gone from being one of the best players in the league to not playing at all. It was devastating. I remember coming home from practice in tears thinking, why can't I just have the chance to show what I can do?

I could easily have used this as an excuse to quit, but I didn't. I kept showing up to every practice and every game, and I sat on the bench.

Then, in one of our final games, we were playing in the state tournament. We were losing—by a lot, and it didn't look like we had any hope at all.

When the coach had pitched everybody on the team and I was the last one sitting on the bench, he finally said, "It's your turn."

My dad recalls looking at the opponents' bench and seeing the frightened faces of the players as, one by one, I struck every single one of them out. I had finally gotten my opportunity, and I wasn't going to be denied.

In the next innings, after getting several hits, I ended up hitting a triple to clear the loaded bases and win the game. The players carried me off the field while the fans cheered. I will never forget that day.

It was a life-changing event for me. A drive was created inside of me to keep going and never quit.

Once I set my mind to fulfilling my calling of helping people heal, I have never stopped. I'm always trying to do better, and I never want to sit on the bench again.

I wrote this book because I want you to experience what it's like to be thankful every day of your life. I want you to have a better understanding of who you are, how your body works, and how to maintain it for peak performance.

God has blessed each and every one of us with an amazing machine. I have found that when we honor God by being thankful for our blessings and taking care of our machines, we receive all the support we need to live our lives with passion and purpose.

I have done my best to present this material in a way that is straightforward, easy to understand, and even fun to read. I want you to enjoy the journey as you read each chapter, go through the discussion questions with your teacher or group leader, and stretch yourself a little by doing the exercises and then sharing what you wrote.

In writing this book, I let God lead the way. I invite you to do the same as you read these words and implement what you learn.

Your Body, God, and You

> *"I will praise thee,*
> *for I am fearfully and wonderfully made.*
> *Marvelous are thy works,*
> *and that my soul knoweth right well."*
> *(Psalms 139:14)*

Who You Are

If I were to ask you, "Who are you?" what would your answer be? Would you tell me your name? Would you describe yourself as a boy or girl, an adult or child, an American or other nationality, or a human being? Or, would you tell me that you are a creation of God?

What if I told you that God has a plan for you and wants you to be happy and healthy so you can fulfill that plan, and what if I could teach you how to naturally be healthy and happy, starting right now, and you could be that way for the rest of your life? Would you want to know more?

A Positive Attitude

Believe it or not, one of the first things that determines your health and happiness is your attitude. If you could be positive at all times, your body would be free from the stress of worry and doubt, creating a natural tendency toward good health.

Unfortunately, keeping up a positive attitude is not always easy. Negativity is all around, and no matter who you are, you're going to be challenged by negative influences and will undoubtedly have bad days. Rising to the challenge of staying positive will ensure that the machine God gave you can function at full capacity.

What God Wants

Do you know what God wants you to do? God wants you to forget about all the things that feel bad and dodge any arrows you may feel are being shot at you. God wants you to move forward in your life and keep your focus on the miraculous machine that you are moving around in.

God also wants you to be thankful. When you remember to be thankful, God will bless you every day. Keep in mind that it is easier to be positive when your machine is running at full capacity and not sputtering. The easiest way to stay positive is to focus on living here on planet Earth and the opportunity God has given you.

How Your Body Works

The way God made your machine is that everything in your body is based on your brain. The brain's connection to your body parts is what keeps you healthy. The better your body is communicating with itself—whether it is from cell to cell or from your brain to every part of your body—the better your machine will function.

> The most important system in the human body is the nervous system. It is the communication system for your body. Every part of your body has a nerve connection to your brain. If you wiggle your foot, for example, that movement starts in the brain.

The better the connection between the brain and a particular body part, the less disease you will have in that body part and the better that body part will function. This holds true for every part in the human body. The better connected your brain is to every single part of your body, the less disease happens.

Disconnection

At any given time, the signal between your brain and a body part—like your arm, wrist, or finger—may be weakened. Some signs of a weak connection are clearly visible. Everybody can see when a person has a limp and is not walking properly or that a person is sitting in a wheelchair and can't stand up.

> Many signs of weakness, however, are not visible. When athletes are not performing at their highest level, they may have no idea that their body is weak because they have no visible signs of weakness.

You Are What You Eat

Besides staying positive, how can you influence your body's ability to maintain strong connections to your brain through your nervous system?

For a long time, it was thought that genetics was primarily responsible for a person's overall health—that diseases were passed down from generation to generation. We now know that genetics plays only about a twenty-five percent role in the disconnection between your brain and any of your body parts. So, what about the other seventy-five percent?

To a large extent, what you put into your body determines the outcome. Here's a simple way to look at it. When your car is on empty, you stop at a gas station and fill it up with gas. After you leave the gas station, if your car starts to sputter and it won't stop sputtering, I guarantee you will never go back to that gas station again.

Food is the fuel that keeps your machine running smoothly. If you know that the foods you are eating are not good for you, and you continue to eat the same foods, you cannot expect your body to maintain a high performance level.

In our present time, people who are twenty years old and younger in the United States have the worst neurology (nervous system function) in the history of the world for that age. The biggest reason for this problem is bad food. We could take a person who is sixty years old and put him or her side by side with someone who is fifteen years old, and the fifteen-year-old would have worse neurology.

God's Healing Machine

You are walking around in a healing machine that has been programmed by God to process certain foods, and God gave you the formula to eat all those foods. When you were born, did you have to learn how to digest a carbohydrate? This process is innate in the machine that God designed for you.

God has included the written software for every type of God-made food within your machine. God has, in fact, given you a computer that has been pre-programmed with all the software you will ever need for your own use. When you enter man-made food—which the software is not designed to process—into your computer, the software is corrupted and weakens.

As you continue is this book, you will learn more about how your body works, how to tell the difference between God-made foods and man-made foods, and why it's so important to respect and maintain God's amazing machine.

Discussion

How happy and healthy are you right now, and what could you do to improve that?

What do you think God's plan for you is, and how do you imagine yourself fulfilling that plan?

What gets in the way of you staying positive, and how can you practice having a more positive attitude?

What do you like most about your life?

What are some examples of how your body is connected to your brain through your nervous system?

What are some signs of a weak connection between your brain and your body?

What foods are you eating that you know are not good for you?

What foods are you eating that you know are good for you?

Discussion Notes

_____

_____

_____

_____

_____

_____

_____

_____

_____

_____

_____

_____

_____

_____

_____

_____

_____

_____

_____

_____

_____

_____

_____

_____

_____

_____

_____

_____

_____

_____

_____

Exercises

Make a list of at least twenty things you are thankful for.

_____

_____

_____

_____

_____

_____

_____

_____

_____

_____

_____

_____

_____

_____

_____

_____

_____

_____

_____

_____

_____

_____

_____

_____

_____

_____

_____

_____

_____

_____

Write a description, from your imagination, of the best God-made food. Describe what it would look like, smell like, taste like, how you would feel when you ate it, and what it would do to your body.

_____

_____

_____

_____

_____

_____

_____

_____

_____

_____

_____

_____

_____

_____

_____

_____

Sharing

Take turns sharing the things you've written in the previous exercises.

_____

_____

_____

_____

_____

_____

_____

_____

_____

_____

_____

_____

_____

_____

_____

_____

_____

_____

_____

_____

_____

_____

_____

_____

_____

_____

_____

_____

_____

_____

God is Love

> *"Whoever does not love*
> *does not know God,*
> *because God is love."*
> *(1 John 4:8)*

Your Ultimate Creator

From the moment you are brought into this world, you have an ultimate creator—beyond your parents—and that creator is God. There is nobody in the world who loves you more than God.

God brought you into this world, gave you an amazing machine, and gave you all the programming in your machine. God is the reason you are reading this book—the reason you can hear, see, touch, feel, smell, and taste. God gave you the ability to breathe, move, and think. God gave you your imagination, your passion, and your intuition.

Love and Fear

So, if God is the one who loves us the most in the world, why doesn't everyone love God the most? People fall short of loving God the most because, as they go through life, they forget the simple fact that God is love and represents love. Instead, people react to man-made influences and fall into fear.

You can classify all emotions as either loving or fearful. Loving emotions are the ones that feel good. Fearful emotions are the ones that feel bad. For example, anger is a form of fear, and joy is a form of love. People who live their lives with more love than fear are healthier and happier than those who are stuck in the fearful emotions.

Overcoming Drama

But how do you stay in the love when the world feels scary and dramatic? Whether it's a negative news report or a difficult personal experience, the circumstances of life can lead you to get caught up in emotional extremes.

If you let them, these obstacles will overshadow and cloud your ability to fall back into love with God. The more you tap into love, the more you are going to be thankful for what you have.

Choosing How You Feel

Being thankful means letting go of anger about your circumstances and instead, being in love with what you currently have. If you broke your arm, would you be thankful that your body is capable of healing the broken bone and that you still have use of your other arm in the meantime, or would you be resentful or angry that the broken bone was going to keep you from doing things you wanted to do? A lot of people would be angry and resentful, but let me ask you, which emotion do you think would feel better—resentful or thankful?

Being thankful also means letting go of fear and trusting that things will get better. If you were diagnosed with a disease, you would have the choice—each and every day—to either be fearful or faithful. You could either keep focusing on the worst thing that could happen, or you could trust that the machine God gave you has been programmed perfectly and knows how to get well. You could also choose to trust that no matter what kind of limitation you might have at any given time, there are still lots of things you can do to be happy, fulfill your purpose, and make a difference in other people's lives.

The more thankful you are to God every minute of every day for everything you have in your amazing machine, the more God will bless you and your machine each and every day.

Knowing How to Pray

Prayer is wonderful, but do you know the best way to pray? If you are asking for things you don't have more than you are thanking God for what you do have, you might want to try it the other way around.

> Imagine children asking their parents for something they really want— something that everybody else has and they don't—and they keep asking over and over, "Please can I have it? Please can I have it? Please can I have it?" If the children do this one time, they might just get what they want, but if they keep nagging and never seem to appreciate what has already been given to them, how do you think their parents will feel about giving them more?

I want you to think of God in the same way. God loves to know how much you appreciate what you have been given.

God Will Bless You

When you pray to God, say, "Thank you so much for my ability to talk to you today, for my family and friends, the food on my plate, the roof over my head, and for my ability to be a friend, digest my food, and walk around today." Thank God every day for those things, and then if you still want to, you can ask for something for yourself or for another person.

Focus more on loving God, appreciating God in your life, and how much God has given you every single minute of every single day, and God will bless you like you have never been blessed before.

Discussion

In what ways do you most feel God's love for you?

What are some unique personal examples of the programming God gave your machine?

What things get in the way of you loving God the most, and how could you turn them around?

What are some examples of fearful emotions and loving emotions?

*What types of drama lead you
to emotional extremes,
and what helps you tap back into love?*

*Have you ever made a choice to feel good
even though your circumstances
were not to your liking?*

*What situations in your life
give you the opportunity
to either be fearful or faithful,
and which do you usually choose?*

*How often do you remember to thank God
for what you have been given,
and how do you feel when you do?*

Discussion Notes

_____

_____

_____

_____

_____

_____

_____

_____

_____

_____

_____

_____

_____

_____

_____

_____

Exercises

> Make a list of things in your life that you have taken for granted—abilities and privileges you have that others may not have—and write a prayer thanking God for all those blessings.

_____

_____

_____

_____

_____

_____

_____

_____

_____

_____

_____

_____

_____

_____

_____

_____

_____

_____

_____

_____

_____

_____

_____

_____

_____

_____

Make a list of people in your life you have taken for granted, and write what you appreciate most about each of them.

_____

_____

_____

_____

_____

_____

_____

_____

_____

_____

_____

_____

_____

_____

_____

_____

Sharing

Take turns sharing the things you've written in the previous exercises.

_____

_____

_____

_____

_____

_____

_____

_____

_____

_____

_____

_____

_____

_____

_____

_____

_____

_____

_____

_____

_____

_____

_____

_____

_____

_____

_____

_____

God is Light

Where is God?

God gave you this amazing machine, and obviously your parents had something to do with it as well. Your mother may have given you her half, and your father may have given you his half, which resulted in this new machine that does not match anybody else's machine in the world.

Your parents (biological or otherwise) are clearly visible. You can see them with your own eyes, and you may even be able to recognize the resemblance you have to them.

But how can you see God? Could your originator—your ultimate creator—be visible in your life as well? And if so, how might you be able to recognize your resemblance to God?

The Light of the World

You've probably seen references in the Bible to God being the "light of the world." That sounds very nice, but did you ever think about what it really means?

You can see light, can't you? It's all around you. It shines down from the sun, and is generated in the world through the power of electricity. In fact, everything you see with your eyes is a reflection of light.

The Speed of Light

If you study the science of light, you will discover that light travels at

671,000,000 miles per hour. Can you
even conceive of how fast that is?

> You see vehicles on the highway traveling
> at 60 or 70 miles per hour. At a car race
> you can see drivers traveling at 200
> miles per hour. You can look up in the
> sky and see an airplane traveling at 500
> miles per hour. When a space shuttle
> goes beyond its orbit of the earth, it
> travels at 24,000 miles per hour.

As you can see, these numbers are not
even close to the speed of light.

Light is Good for You

Even though you may not be able to
conceive of the speed of light, you can
certainly see the effects of light in your
life. From your eyesight, to your body
temperature, to your connection with
other people and things, light is a major
factor in the operation of your machine.

Humans would not survive if light was taken away from the earth. In fact, most living organisms would not survive without light. Light is good for you.

Light is Your Source of Power

I want you to think about light being God every time you see it. Light is around you and within you as your source of power. Imagine how much power is generated at 671,000,000 miles per hour!

That is the power of God, and you have that power available to you every moment of every day. Just imagine what you can accomplish with all that power! God gives you that power so you can use it. How will you use it today?

Discussion

In what ways do you resemble your parents?

In what ways do you resemble God?

What does it mean to you that God is the "light of the world?"

How do you see God's light reflected in the world?

What are the fastest things you can think of,
and how do they compare
to the speed of light?

What are some of the effects
of light in your life?

Why is light so important to our survival?

Where do you see God's power around you?

When do you most feel God's
power within you?

Discussion Notes

_____

_____

_____

_____

_____

_____

_____

_____

_____

_____

_____

_____

_____

_____

_____

Exercises

> Close your eyes, listen, and follow along in your imagination as your teacher or group leader reads out loud the instructions below.

(Read SLOWLY and gently, pausing between phrases.)

"Imagine yourself being filled up with light from above...the brilliant and beautiful light of God...coming down through your head...filling up your heart...moving into every part of your body...out to your arms and hands... down through your torso into your belly...down through your legs and feet."

"Feel that light in your body...feel the heat and the energy...feel the power and the potential...feel the love and the peace...feel the wisdom and connection."

"Now, imagine that beautiful, brilliant light of God radiating out from your body to everyone and everything around you...filling the room with light...and then expanding out to the rest of the building...filling the building with God's light...and then expanding further out into the community...filling everyone and everything with its power and radiance...and then continuing to expand out into the rest of the world... touching the whole planet...filling it with light and love...and then expanding even further to encompass the entire universe...filling every corner of creation with its brilliance and power."

"Take another moment to feel the light energy in your body...coming from God...moving through your heart... and connecting to everything in the universe. Notice how that feels. And when you are ready, open your eyes, and write about your experience."

_____

_____

_____

_____

_____

_____

_____

_____

_____

_____

_____

_____

_____

_____

_____

_____

Make a list of all the things you could do with your God power and how each of those things would make a difference in the world.

_____

_____

_____

_____

_____

_____

_____

_____

_____

_____

_____

_____

_____

_____

_____

_____

_____

_____

_____

_____

_____

_____

_____

_____

_____

_____

_____

_____

_____

_____

Sharing

Take turns sharing the things you've written in the previous exercises.

_____

_____

_____

_____

_____

_____

_____

_____

_____

_____

_____

_____

_____

_____

_____

_____

_____

_____

_____

_____

_____

_____

_____

_____

_____

_____

_____

_____

_____

_____

The Nervous System
Part I

> *"And be not conformed to this world:*
> *but be ye transformed*
> *by the renewing of your mind..."*
> *(Romans 12)*

Connection

Have you ever heard it said that your finger bone is connected to your hand bone, your hand bone is connected to your arm bone, and so on? Well, the machine that God has given you is much more complex than that, and I'm going to do my best to give you a better understanding of it, while still keeping it simple.

The most important part of your machine is your nervous system. This system is comprised of your brain, your spinal cord, and all of the nerves coming off of them and going to all parts of your body. To achieve the most from this amazing machine that God has provided, you need to focus your attention on your nervous system as much as possible.

Communication

God designed your machine to communicate. For example, the better the communication between your brain and your foot, the stronger the bones, muscles, lymphatic system, and blood vessels in your foot will be.

That's how your nervous system works. It's the controller for your entire body. It's the first system your body makes as an embryo, and it's the last system of your body to die. When your nervous system starts, your life begins, and when it fails, your life is over.

Blood Flow

God's machine is programmed perfectly. Every part of your body—your skin, bones, organs, muscles, and every single blood vessel—must have a connection to your brain, which is the central part of your nervous system.

Did you know that you have smooth muscles inside of each blood vessel that contract and pump your blood to every part of your body and then back to your heart? Every part of every blood vessel has an individual nerve connection to the brain.

Digestion

From the moment you swallow something, to the moment it leaves your body, there is roughly a mile of tubing, and every section of that tubing must have a nerve connection to your brain in order for it to function. Every part of your gastrointestinal tract (stomach, pancreas, large and small intestines, etc.) relies on its connection to the brain.

> When the lines of communication are clear, your stomach can shout out to the brain, "Hey, I need something!" and your brain can respond, "Okay, here you go." If the connection is not functioning properly, the stomach can be hollering for what it needs, but the portal does not receive the signal, and the brain is unable to process the request.

This is a classic example of how your nervous system can be weak, and you have no idea that there is a problem. It is vitally important that you keep your nervous system connected.

Processes

Every day of your life, your amazing machine provides you with the ability to perform millions and millions of processes. Many of these processes are automatic and happen without your awareness, like the production of particular digestive enzymes when you eat, or specific amounts of hormones that other body systems need. Other processes—such as looking at someone, moving a body part, or participating in an event—are consciously chosen with your full awareness.

The machine that God designed for you is an absolutely magnificent creation. Man will never have the capacity to invent any machine even remotely as powerful as yours.

Discussion

> *What kinds of connections are you aware of in your body, and what part do you think your nervous system plays in those connections?*

> *What are some of the ways in which the parts of your body communicate with each other?*

> *What are some of the benefits of having each and every blood vessel individually connected to your brain?*

What are some examples of clear communication between your digestive system and your brain, and how do they benefit you?

What are some examples of poor communication between your digestive system and your brain, and how do they limit you?

What are some examples of your body's unconscious processes?

What are some examples of your body's conscious processes?

Discussion Notes

Exercises

> Think about what choices in your
> daily life might keep your nervous
> system strong, and write a list of
> some of the ways you could do
> that.

_____

_____

_____

_____

_____

_____

_____

_____

_____

_____

_____

_____

Imagine that you are a member of an alien species studying God's amazing human machine, and write about your discoveries.

_____

_____

_____

_____

_____

_____

_____

_____

_____

_____

_____

_____

_____

Sharing

Take turns sharing the things you've written in the previous exercises.

_____

_____

_____

_____

_____

_____

_____

_____

_____

_____

_____

_____

_____

_____

_____

_____

_____

_____

_____

_____

_____

_____

_____

_____

_____

_____

The Nervous System
Part II

> *"...your bodies are temples of the Holy Spirit...whom you have received from God... Therefore honor God with your bodies."*
> *(1 Corinthians 6:19-20)*

Endocrine System

Your entire metabolism and hormone system are known as your endocrine system. Your hormones are not produced by just one gland; they are produced by a big baseball team of glands that God has assembled.

God had to develop the body this way, because hormones control so many different body responses. When the alternator in your car goes out, your car dies, because you have only one alternator. If you had only one gland that produced all your hormones, you'd be in big trouble if that gland failed.

God designed your machine with back-ups (and multiple back-ups in most cases). You can live without a gall bladder or other organs, and you can live without certain muscles and still accomplish the same range of motion, because there are back-ups designed to perform the same functions.

The endocrine system is not only very complex, it's also a simple group of glands and organs that produce all of your hormones *and* regulate your metabolism, so it's important to keep them all connected.

Lymphatic System

Your lymphatic system is a network of tubes that run throughout your entire body. These tubes are separate from the vessels that carry your blood. Inside the tubes you have lymph, a fluid-based waste that the system filters out when you breathe.

> The foremost way your body detoxifies is by breathing. That's why exercise is so helpful; it forces you to breathe in and out more. Without exercise, the average person breathes in and out 23,000 times a day, while the person who exercises breathes in and out 40,000 times a day.

The way God designed your machine is that every part of your lymphatic system must have an individual nerve connection to the brain. Isn't your body amazing?

Immune System

What if I told you that your immune system is like the CIA?

When the U.S. president goes out in public, the CIA's job is to scan the crowd, identify potential threats, and keep them from attacking the president. To ensure safety, every agent is equipped with a communication device which keeps them all connected.

When someone sitting next to you sneezes or coughs, a crowd of germs is released into the air and onto surrounding surfaces. If and when you come into contact with these germs, your immune system's job is to identify potential threats to your body's health and keep them from attacking your system.

As long as there is good communication between your immune system and your nervous system, your brain will know what to let in and what to kick out. That's why it is crucial for each individual nerve connection to remain strong.

Muscular System

When you move the muscles of your hand, foot, neck, or any other body part, you are moving those parts by your skeletal muscles, and in fact, by your nervous system because of the connection it has to your skeletal muscles. Your brain is giving you power, through your nervous system, to move all those body parts.

> The act of kicking your leg out isn't accomplished by your quadriceps muscle alone. What happens if I cut the nerve that runs from your quadriceps muscle to your brain? Even though the muscle is still sitting right there, you will never kick that leg out again. When the connection to the brain was severed, so was the power.

You can lose power whether the connection is visible or not. While it is obviously crucial for athletes to keep their nervous systems connected to all of their skeletal muscles, isn't it just as important for you?

Respiratory System

God designed the respiratory system to take in adequate nutrients. You can do without eating and drinking for a while, but you must breathe in order to survive. What you breathe in will change depending on conditions like your environment and the time of year.

> Oxygen is the most prevalent element in the chemical composition of your machine, and for every breath you take, your respiratory system is capable of getting the right amount of oxygen into your lungs and depositing it into your blood. It's an amazing process that your machine is programmed to do.

Your nerves are wired to your lungs and airways and the muscles responsible for pulling air in and pushing air out of your body. The better the wiring is to the brain, the more capable you are of ingesting the proper amount of oxygen in any environment. If you're having trouble breathing, there could be a disconnection in those pathways that needs to be addressed.

Reproductive System

The reproductive system does what the name implies; it reproduces. In this amazing process, God gives us the ability to combine our own seed with someone else's seed.

> Unless you have an identical twin, there is nobody else in the entire world who matches the DNA God has given you. Each of your parents is roughly 50 percent matched to you, and your siblings are about 70 percent. Nobody else matches you at all, unless they're related to you, and the likenesses decrease with each generation of relationship.

Isn't it amazing that nobody else has your same body parts? God designed every part of every system in your body specifically for you. Since you can't just go to a parts store and ask for a kidney to replace your kidney that isn't functioning very well, wouldn't your best option be to honor God by taking care of all the parts you've been given?

Discussion

What are some of your body's responses
that are controlled by hormones
through the endocrine system?

In what ways are you supporting your
lymphatic system to detoxify your body,
and how could you do even better?

What are some things you are doing
to keep your immune system strong,
and what else could you do?

What evidence do you see
that your nervous system
is connected to your muscles?

What musculoskeletal processes and activities are most important to you, and why?

What are some conditions of your environment, or the time of year, that can change what you are breathing in?

Discussion Notes

_____

_____

_____

_____

_____

_____

_____

_____

_____

_____

_____

_____

_____

_____

_____

_____

_____

_____

Exercises

> List some ways that you can honor God by taking better care of the amazing machine you've been given.

_____

_____

_____

_____

_____

_____

_____

_____

_____

_____

_____

_____

Write about some of the amazing things you could accomplish in your life if you always keep your machine in excellent condition.

_____

_____

_____

_____

_____

_____

_____

_____

_____

_____

_____

_____

Sharing

Take turns sharing the things you've written in the previous exercises.

_____

_____

_____

_____

_____

_____

_____

_____

_____

_____

_____

_____

_____

_____

_____

_____

_____

_____

_____

_____

_____

_____

_____

_____

_____

_____

_____

_____

_____

Interference

> "But the fruit of the Spirit is love, joy, peace,
> forbearance, kindness, goodness,
> faithfulness, gentleness and self-control.
> Against such things there is no law."
> (Galatians 5:22-23)

Choices and Actions

Now that you know how important it is
to keep a strong connection between
your nervous system and all the other
systems in your body, how are you
going to do that? And if God designed
your machine in such an amazing way,
why doesn't it just work perfectly all the
time? What gets in the way?

God's job was to create your machine, and your job is to keep it as healthy as possible so it will continue running at full capacity. God gave you free will, so you get to choose how you want to live.

Of course, everyone else was also given free will, and unless you make conscious decisions about your health and happiness, the actions of others can have a big influence on your quality of life. When they don't support your well-being, these influences are known as interference.

Awareness and Intuition

Take a look at your life right now. Do the actions of the people around you always serve your best interests, or are you being influenced in ways that may be weakening your machine?

How about the news media and commercial advertising? Could they be having a negative impact on you without you even realizing it?

God gave you some powerful tools for answering those questions: your awareness and your intuition. You can use these tools to tell you which people, places, activities, drinks, foods, and other substances to include in your life and which ones to stay away from because they are not good for your energy. For example, anything that you rub onto your skin or breathe into your body can either positively or negatively affect your nerves, and your awareness and intuition can help you determine what's right or wrong for you.

Intention

Although awareness and intuition must be developed and nurtured in order to work properly, this may be the opposite of what you experience as you grow up. When children complain of aches, pains, or discomforts (real nerve problems), well-meaning adults and peers often say things like "suck it up," "don't be a crybaby," or "stop being such a hypochondriac." Another common response is to use over-the-counter medications to alleviate symptoms instead of learning how to recognize and repair the underlying nerve problem.

Developing and nurturing your intuition and awareness is all about intention. When you decide you want to use these faculties more, God will automatically support you in getting better and better at it.

The Power of Influence

If you have been hanging around with someone who is influencing you to do things that are not God-like, that's interference. What do you think would happen if you either stopped hanging around with that person or stopped allowing them to influence you in a negative way and started influencing them in a positive way instead?

> You have the God-given power to influence and to be influenced. When you choose to hang around with people who influence you in positive ways, your life gets better and you make an even greater impact on the lives of others.

The Power of Food

God made fuel for your machine in the form of naturally grown foods and pure water. Since your body was designed to use these foods and water as fuel, it recognizes them and knows exactly what to do with them.

> Artificial ingredients and processes, on the other hand, are not recognized by your body as fuel and can keep it from functioning at its full capacity.

So, how do you know if something is artificial? Can you just go to the store, read the label on the package, and as long as you see the word "natural" you can be confident that it will be good for you?

Food Labels

No matter what it says on the label, many packaged foods contain artificial ingredients and are processed using unnatural methods. Even the fresh fruits and vegetables you get in the store may have been grown using artificial processes that alter their biological structure so your body does not recognize them as fuel.

Unless you plant your own garden with God-made seeds and drink water from your own spring or well, you will need to do more than just read labels to ensure that what you put in your body will support your machine as God intended.

God's Guidance

With all these man-made ingredients and processes disguised as God-made natural foods, how can you follow God's plan and fuel your machine properly so it will function at full capacity?

> The best thing you can do is to ask questions, learn as much as you can about the foods you eat, and make the healthiest choices you possibly can. Your body will give you feedback about how you're doing and God will guide you, through your intuition, to the information and resources that are best for you.

Invisible Interference

Besides the influences of people, foods, and the media, did you know that you are also being affected by interferences that you cannot even see? From thoughts and emotions, to computers and electrical devices, everything around you and within you has a frequency that influences your machine.

> Your cell phone is a perfect example. It emits radio waves that are invisible, just like microwaves, and can interfere with your brain's capacity to communicate with its parts.

When you board a plane, you are told to turn your cell phone off to keep the waves emitting from the computer in your cell phone from interfering with the big computer on the plane. In the same way, you can protect your machine from cell phone interference by using a headset and by moving your cell phone around so that you don't have it directly on you at all times.

Maintaining Your Machine

Your body was designed to repair itself and does not require any artificial substances to maintain it. Being aware of where the interference is and listening to your intuition will help you to keep God's machine functioning at peak levels in order to carry out what God has planned for you.

When you follow God's guidance and fuel your machine for optimal performance, breakdowns are much less likely to occur and much easier to manage when they do occur. Simple adjustments can bring you right back to the fully functioning powerhouse you were designed to be.

Discussion

> *What free will choices are you making that support your health and happiness?*

> *In what ways are you allowing the actions of others to influence you, and what are the results?*

> *In what ways are you allowing the news media and commercial advertising to influence you?*

> *How are you using your awareness and intuition to support your choices?*

How are you using your
God-given power to influence others?

What are some artificial ingredients and
processes your body might not recognize
as fuel?

What questions can you ask and
what sources can you go to for
information about the foods you eat?

What invisible frequencies could be
influencing your machine, and
what could you do to minimize
their effects?

Discussion Notes

_____

_____

_____

_____

_____

_____

_____

_____

_____

_____

_____

_____

_____

_____

_____

Exercises

> Make a list of people who
> influence you in a negative way,
> and a list of people who influence
> you in a positive way.

_____

_____

_____

_____

_____

_____

_____

_____

_____

_____

_____

_____

> Write a sample journal entry from the perspective of someone (real or imaginary) who has been positively influenced by you. Pretend you are them writing about you and describing what you have done, how it has affected them, and how thankful they are to have you in their life.

_____

_____

_____

_____

_____

_____

_____

_____

_____

_____

Sharing

Take turns sharing the things you've written in the previous exercises.

_____

_____

_____

_____

_____

_____

_____

_____

_____

_____

_____

Your Will and Determination

> "I have set before you life and death,
> blessings and curses. Now choose life..."
> (Deuteronomy 30:19)

Desire

God pre-programmed every detail of
your amazing machine, and then gave
you the power to choose how to use it.
By activating this power through your
will and determination, you get to co-
create your life with God.

You have a desire, deep within you, that
is uniquely yours. As you develop your
desire and share it with others, you are
completing the most important part

of your machine's programming, and commencing the fulfillment of God's plan.

Passion

My deepest desire, ever since I was a child, has been to help people with their health and to make them feel better. This deeply-rooted passion is always within me, and when I'm working, I don't feel as if I'm working; I am just here to help people.

Do you know what your greatest passion is? An easy way to discover it is to look at your life, and notice what feels the best to you and what you're really good at.

Action

One day, when I was about ten years old, my great grandmother was suffering from a massive headache. I wanted to help rid her of the headache, so I rubbed and touched various spots on her head.

This was the beginning of me acting on my desire to help others.

> As I developed that desire, I discovered methods of helping people that I really enjoyed, and ways to make my work more and more effective. Because I used the free will that God gave me to discover my passion and act on it, people all over the world are choosing to follow my methods and suggestions to improve their nerve health, and are therefore changing the quality of their lives.

Life Purpose

No matter who you are or where you're from, God has a purpose for you and wants you to discover it. You can do this by noticing what makes your clock tick— what motivates you to do something because it feels important.

> Whether your purpose is big or small, it's the perfect size for you. You may prefer the consistency of doing the same thing

every day, or have a complex vision to change the world. Just follow your passion, and God will let you know that you're on track.

Being Your Best

God wants you to be the best person that you can be. When you are willing to dig deep inside yourself, God will help you find your talents and abilities and make the most of them.

Do you want your life to be hard or easy? Taking good care of the machine that God gave you will make it much easier for you to do all the good things that God designed you to be able to do.

Success

Who is responsible for success in your life? Are you allowing the influences of people or circumstances to determine your success, or are you using your free

will and determination in partnership
with God?

How far do you think you can go? When
you maintain your machine and follow
God's plan, there are *no limits* to what
you can do. It's all up to you!

Discussion

> *What is your deepest desire, and how can you develop that desire and share it with others?*

> *What comes easy to you, feels good, and you are really good at it?*

> *In what ways are you acting on your desire and passion, and how could you do more of that?*

> *What motivates you and feels important to you?*

Do you have a simple purpose or a complex vision?

When you are following your passion, in what ways does God let you know that you're on track?

What talents and abilities do you have, and how can you make it easier for your machine to do those things?

How can you use your free will and determination in partnership with God?

Discussion Notes

_____

_____

_____

_____

_____

_____

_____

_____

_____

_____

_____

_____

_____

_____

_____

Exercises

> Make a list of all your talents and abilities, and for each one, write down how you could support your machine to improve your performance.

_____

_____

_____

_____

_____

_____

_____

_____

_____

_____

Imagine what it would be like if there were no limits to your success. Write about what you would do, and describe how it would feel to do it.

_____

_____

_____

_____

_____

_____

_____

_____

_____

_____

_____

Sharing

Take turns sharing the things you've written in the previous exercises.

_____

_____

_____

_____

_____

_____

_____

_____

_____

_____

_____

Conclusion

I'd like to thank you and acknowledge you for reading this book and being open to the ideas and information I have presented. I am very passionate about what I do and how I can help people be healthier and happier by sharing what I have learned.

In this book, I have given you a very brief overview of God's amazing machine, how it works, and why it's so important to respect and maintain it for your best performance. If you liked what you read here, I invite you to learn more by visiting my website, www.NerveHealth.com, and reading my book, *The Hidden Diagnosis*.

Now that you've come to the end of the book, it's time for you to decide what's next for you. How can you take what you've learned here and use it to make your life better? How can you use your God-given power to influence others in a more positive way? Who can you share this information with?

The decisions you make are important, and the actions you take really do have an impact—not just on you, but on those around you and even on those far away from you. Always remember that when you make the choice to do good things for yourself and others, God supports you and blesses you.

I wish you all the best, and I look forward to connecting with you again in the future.

Dr. Chris Cormier
www.NerveHealth.com
Founder of the Nerve Health Institute

About The Author

Dr. Chris Cormier graduated from Louisiana State University in 1994 with a Bachelor of Science degree in Kinesiology. He continued his education at Texas Chiropractic College in Houston, where he was a member of the Omega Psi Honors Fraternity and received his Doctorate of Chiropractic with Honors in 1998. He is a licensed Chiropractic Physician in Louisiana and a member of the Chiropractic Association of Louisiana. He is also an affiliate of the American Chiropractic Association.

Since finishing chiropractic school, Dr. Chris has continued to search the world for the best and most innovative ways to help the human body. As a chiropractic physician in Lafayette, Louisiana since 1999, he has helped thousands of people to live healthier lives. People travel from all over the country to seek his care.

He is also proud to say that he is one of the pioneers in the most amazing nervous system rehabilitation technique ever invented, Quantum Neurology®, whereby he has been given numerous awards, including his work on restoring the nerve connections between the brain and the organs in the human body.

Additionally, Dr. Chris invented two nutritional products, SuperfruitsGT and Chiropractor's Choice, which are currently distributed throughout the United States.

SuperfruitsGT is the strongest, all whole food, anti-aging antioxidant liquid on the market today, and it is the best way to start your day.

Chiropractor's Choice is a capsule combination of the world's best whole foods to support normal low levels of inflammation, pain, and arthritis.

Dr. Chris is also the author of a book entitled, *The Hidden Diagnosis: What Doctors Are Missing and Why You Should Know*.

Helping people is truly his calling, and he works tirelessly at helping everyone with whom he comes into contact.

Finally, and most importantly, Dr. Chris has been married to his wife, Missy, for more than 16 years and they are the proud parents of Hayden, Molly, and Lucas.

29016963R00085

Printed in Great Britain
by Amazon